ICE AGE 2
THE MELTDOWN

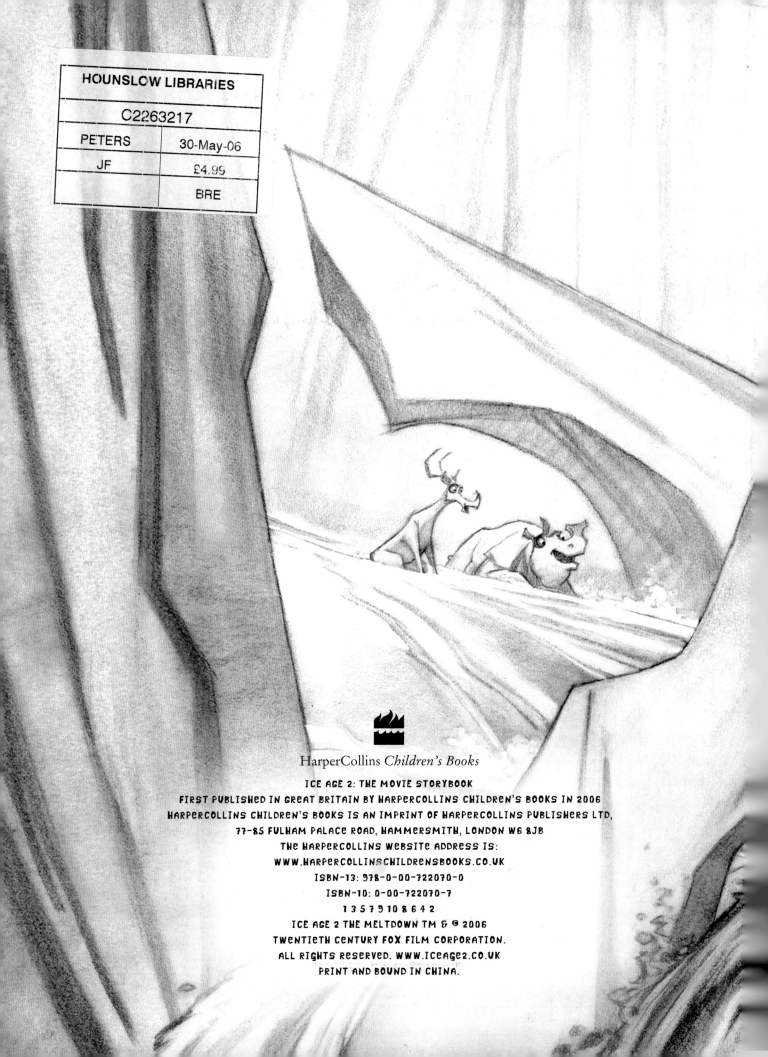

HarperCollins *Children's Books*

ICE AGE 2: THE MOVIE STORYBOOK
FIRST PUBLISHED IN GREAT BRITAIN BY HARPERCOLLINS CHILDREN'S BOOKS IN 2006
HARPERCOLLINS CHILDREN'S BOOKS IS AN IMPRINT OF HARPERCOLLINS PUBLISHERS LTD,
77-85 FULHAM PALACE ROAD, HAMMERSMITH, LONDON W6 8JB
THE HARPERCOLLINS WEBSITE ADDRESS IS:
WWW.HARPERCOLLINSCHILDRENSBOOKS.CO.UK
ISBN-13: 978-0-00-722070-0
ISBN-10: 0-00-722070-7
1 3 5 7 9 10 8 6 4 2

ICE AGE 2™
THE MELTDOWN

THE MOVIE STORYBOOK

ADAPTED BY
JENNIFER FRANTZ

ILLUSTRATIONS BY
PETER CLARKE

It was a beautiful day in the Valley, and everything was as it should be. The sun was beaming down, families were having fun, and Scrat was chasing down a meal.

And Sid the sloth was getting no respect.

"What's going on here?" Manny the mammoth asked, interrupting a spirited game of Hit-the-Sloth.

Sid looked relieved to see his buddies Manny and Diego the saber-toothed tiger. Like many of Sid's plans, his *Campo del Sid* summer camp wasn't turning out quite as he had imagined.

"I told you, Sid, you're not qualified to run a camp," Manny said as he freed Sid from the clutches of his campers.

Diego agreed. Sid could barely take care of himself, let alone a group of kids.

Sid was hurt by his friends' lack of support.

"You guys never think I can do anything," he said. "I'm an equal member of this herd, you know. You need to start treating me with respect!"

Sid stormed off. Manny and Diego were looking after his campers, when they heard a commotion.

"Fast Tony says the world's gonna flood!" screamed a panicked aardvark. Other animals quickly joined in the hubbub.

Fast Tony was a smooth talker who would do or say *anything* to make a buck. Now he was making up stories about a big flood, just so he could sell special equipment for breathing underwater.

Manny confronted Fast Tony. "Why are you scaring everybody with this doomsday stuff?"

"Haven't you heard?" cried another aardvark. "The ice is melting!"

The crowd continued to argue back and forth until someone screamed, "Look! Some idiot's going down the Eviscerator!" The Eviscerator was the steepest, scariest, tallest, deadliest ice slope around.

"Please tell me it's not our idiot," Manny said aloud. But it was! The idiot was Sid!

Sid had come up with some bad ideas before, but jumping off the Eviscerator to gain some respect was his worst yet. Luckily, his friends were there to save him—again.

Manny snatched Sid up with his trunk just in time, but slipped and fell backwards, sending Diego sliding across the ice. When Diego stood up, the ice around him started to crack. Through the fragile ice, the friends saw water! Diego eyed it anxiously, and then leaped to solid ground.

"You know, if I didn't know you better, Diego, I'd think you were afraid of the water," Sid said.

Diego grabbed him by the throat.

"Okay, okay, good thing I know you better," Sid said.

"Guys, Fast Tony was right," Manny cried. "Everything *is* melting! We've got to warn the others!"

The friends began to make their way across a narrow ice bridge. Suddenly they heard a cracking sound. Then—*whoosh*—the ice gave way! Manny, Sid, and Diego were free-falling at breakneck speed—*down the Eviscerator!*

When the friends landed in a crumpled heap at the bottom, Fast Tony was still addressing the skeptical audience. Suddenly, a voice came from above. It was a lone vulture, perched in a nearby tree.

"Flood's real, alright. And it's coming fast. Ain't no way out. Unless . . . you make it to the end of the Valley. There's a boat. It can save you."

The crowd breathed a collective sigh of relief.

"But ya'll better hurry. Ground's meltin'! In three days' time, the water's gonna hit the geyser fields . . . BOOM!"

Everyone jumped back, terrified. The vulture continued on.

"There is some good news, though . . . the more of you that die, the better I eat."

And with that, he flew off.

Soon all the animals in the Valley were running for their lives. In the midst of the mayhem, a huge ice boulder fell from a melting glacier. Animals screamed in terror and fled, too upset to notice that something inside the boulder had shifted.

"Keep it moving. Keep it moving," Manny called as he tried to direct the traffic.

But everyone was too frantic to pay attention. The Valley was in chaos. Panicked animals hustled this way and that preparing for their journey.

Sid ran up to Manny, his face stuffed with berries. "Manny, Manny. I just heard you're going extinct."

"I am *not* going extinct," Manny replied, furious. But almost as soon as he said it, a family of aardvarks walked by and the father called out "Kids, look! The last mammoth!"

Outside the Valley, Manny, Sid, and Diego stopped for a break from their journey. Manny sat quietly by a river thinking about how his world was changing. He thought about the flood and how long it had been since he'd seen another mammoth.

Maybe it was true—maybe his kind *was* becoming extinct. That's what Sid had been telling him. Manny thought about the family he used to have, his wife and child that had died, and he felt lonely.

"I guess it's just you and me now," he said sadly to his reflection.

Manny's thoughts were interrupted by a loud crack. When he looked up he saw another mammoth hanging from a tree branch. *Boom!* The branch broke and the mammoth tumbled to the ground.

Manny stared for a moment, unable to speak. Then he yelled, "I knew it! I knew I wasn't the only one!"

Manny was excited to find another mammoth, but he soon realized there was something very special about *this* mammoth. Ellie thought she was a possum! She climbed trees, hung upside down, and even played dead.

Ellie introduced Manny, Sid, and Diego to her possum brothers, Crash and Eddie. "I don't think her tree goes all the way to the top branch!" Manny whispered warily to Sid.

But Sid was already hatching a plan. He thought Manny and Ellie should stick together—they might be the only two mammoths left.

"Manny wants me to ask you if you'd like to escape the flood with us," Sid said to Ellie.

Manny tried to protest, but it was too late. Ellie and her brothers agreed to join them. Together the group set out on their long journey.

Traveling through the rapidly melting landscape wasn't easy for the group. Ice crashed down around them, water crept ever-closer, and tempers began to flare.

"Will you cut it out?!" Diego snarled, as Crash and Eddie jumped wildly on the ice. The thought of water below the thin crust of ice was making Diego edgy.

"Cry me a river, blubber-toothed tiger," Crash taunted back.

Diego wasn't the only one who was nervous.

"I've got a really bad feeling about this," Ellie said. "My possum sense is tingling."

Suddenly something crashed through the ice, sending the group flying! It was two prehistoric water reptiles, Cretaceous and Maelstrom. After a few thousand years on ice, they had thawed out and were looking for trouble.

Manny and the gang began scrambling for safety, but Cretaceous and Maelstrom were hot on their tails. They snapped their powerful jaws through the ice just inches from the friends.

After several close calls, the herd was able to shake Cretaceous and Maelstrom. But Manny had a sinking feeling this wasn't the last they'd see of the nasty pair.

As the group journeyed on, Crash and Eddie amused themselves by chasing each other through some woods. Not wanting to miss out on the possum fun, Ellie chased after her brothers. She quickly got stuck under a fallen tree.

Manny's frustration with Ellie had reached its peak. How could she think she was a possum? He marched over to her.

"Don't you think picking them up like *this* would be easier?" Manny said, tossing the tree aside swiftly with his trunk.

But Ellie didn't answer. Something had come over her.

She stood up and started walking. Manny followed.

When Ellie came to a huge meadow, she stopped. A memory washed over her—a memory of herself as a baby, lost and alone. She was curled up under a tree, crying, when a mother possum and her two babies appeared. The possum mom had adopted her and taken care of her. But that didn't make her a possum. Manny was right. She was a mammoth.

"I know this place," Ellie said.

"A mammoth never forgets," Manny whispered.

Exhausted from their travels, the group found a place to camp for the night and drifted off to sleep. But before long, the rock Sid was sleeping on began to move. Sid was being kidnapped!

The next thing he knew, Sid was staring at an entire village of mini-sloths. They fell to their knees and began to bow down to Sid. Then one of them led Sid to a giant sculpture that looked just like him and handed him two rocks.

"Fire-god! Rocks!" the mini-sloth commanded.

Confused, Sid rubbed the rocks together, sending out sparks that quickly turned into flames and raced up the wooden statue. The hordes of mini-sloths cheered wildly!

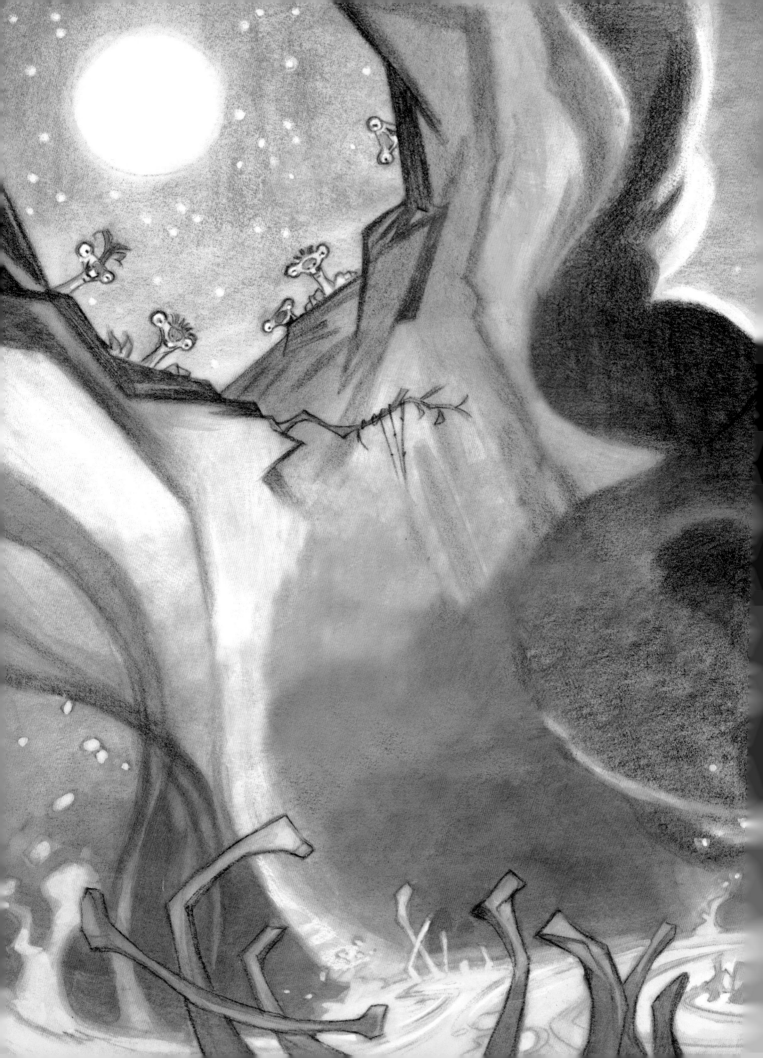

But things soon turned ugly. Sid learned that the mini-sloths knew about the melting ice, too, and they had made their own plan to stop it—sacrificing the Fire-god. And that meant Sid!

Sid suddenly found himself bound by vines and dangling over a fiery tar pit.

"Sacrifice the Fire-god!" the mini-sloths cried, launching Sid into the pit.

Lucky for Sid, no sooner was he hurled into the tar pit than the vines wrapped around him snapped him back up. Then he went down again, then up again, this time covered in tar and dinosaur bones and looking like a monster. The mini-sloths screamed and scattered as the "Sid-o-saur" landed on top of the giant statue.

At the camp the next morning, the group awoke to find water *everywhere*.

Soon they heard the sound of footsteps approaching. It was a sleepy-looking Sid.

"Oh, hi. Hey, you'll never guess what happened to me," he cried. "I was kidnapped by a tribe of mini-sloths!"

The wilder the details of Sid's story got—*Fire-gods, burning idols, tar pits*—the more suspicious his friends grew. Sid had come up with some real doozies before, but this one took the prize.

"Sid, you were dreaming. C'mon," Manny said, leading Sid and the rest of the group on their way. Escaping the flood was more important than listening to one of Sid's crazy stories.

"There it is," Ellie said in awe.

Cresting the top of a tall hill, the group finally saw what they'd been traveling toward—the huge boat perched atop a mountain in the distance.

"We made it!" Diego added. The friends celebrated with a mudball fight. Their journey was almost over.

But the friends soon discovered that reaching the boat would not be easy. *Whoosh!* A geyser exploded a few feet from Manny and Ellie. They were surrounded! Boiling water was shooting up on all sides. Their path was blocked.

The herd looked over the vast geyser field. "There's only one way to go. Straight through," Manny said.

"We'll head back and go around," Ellie decided. "If we go through this, we'll get blown to bits!"

"We go forward!" Manny argued.

"We go back!" Ellie yelled. Unable to agree, Manny and Ellie headed their separate ways. Manny with his herd, and Ellie with hers.

Frustrated, Manny started off through the geyser field, narrowly avoiding the boiling water. Sid and Diego tried their best to keep up, but Manny was far ahead of them. He couldn't stop thinking about his argument with Ellie. Even when the ground split open in front of him, and a wall of boiling water shot up, Manny was still in a daze.

"C'mon Manny! C'mon! Let's go!" Diego yelled.

When Manny looked up, a stream of boiling water was heading straight toward him. Diego ran right into him, pushing him in the right direction.

"That way!" he yelled.

When Manny, Sid, and Diego reached the boat, they anxiously looked for Ellie and the possums. There were panicked animals everywhere, but no sign of Ellie, Crash, or Eddie. To add to the chaos, a fussy bird named Gustav was acting as gatekeeper on the boat. "At this time, we are only boarding animals with mates," he announced haughtily.

"MATES?!" Manny, Sid, and Diego cried. Like many of the other animals, the three friends were mateless. If they couldn't get on the boat, how would they escape the flood?

Meanwhile, things weren't looking much better for Ellie and the possums. The ground continued to rumble, and ice and boulders had crashed down all around them, trapping them inside a cave.

Ellie tried to move the boulder trapping her, but it was no use. It wouldn't budge. Then she noticed a tiny opening that her brothers could fit through. Ellie scooped Crash and Eddie up in her trunk.

"You guys have got to go," she told them. She was stuck, but they could still save themselves.

"Ellie, don't worry, we're going for help!" Eddie cried when they were out of the cave. He and Crash dashed off.

Back at the boat things had gotten worse. The ground was shaking violently, and the dam had given way, unleashing raging floodwaters. All the animals were more panicked than ever.

Crash and Eddie ran through the crowd, dodging animals along the way.

"Manny!" Crash called out.

"It's Ellie!" Eddie said.

"She's trapped in a cave!" Crash added. Without hesitation, Manny ran from the boat and thundered down the hill with Sid, Diego, and the possums.

As the herd rushed across an ice bridge, a huge wave obliterated it, scattering the group. Manny and the possums were swept away with the water, while Sid and Diego watched from an opposite ledge.

The possums clung to a tree in the raging waters, while Manny swam straight for the cave.

Sid jumped headfirst off the ledge to save Crash and Eddie. But he hit his head on a piece of ice and passed out. Now it was up to Diego to save Crash, Eddie, *and* Sid.

Diego was petrified of the water, but he knew this was no time for fear: The others needed him. Psyching himself up, Diego leaped into the raging current.

"Trust your instincts," he told himself, as Sid had told him once before. "Attack the water. I'm stalking the prey."

Diego tiger-paddled his way to the others, flipped Sid onto his back, and grabbed the tree limb the possums were clinging to. He claw-kicked his way safely to shore.

But at the cave, things were getting worse for Ellie. She was still trapped, and the cave was now filling with water. The pocket of air at the top of the cave was growing smaller and smaller every minute.

Manny grabbed a tree and jammed it into the small space Ellie had lifted the possums through. Using all his might, he pushed on the tree, trying to wedge the boulder out. It didn't budge. The water continued to rise, and Ellie had to stick her trunk through the opening in order to breathe.

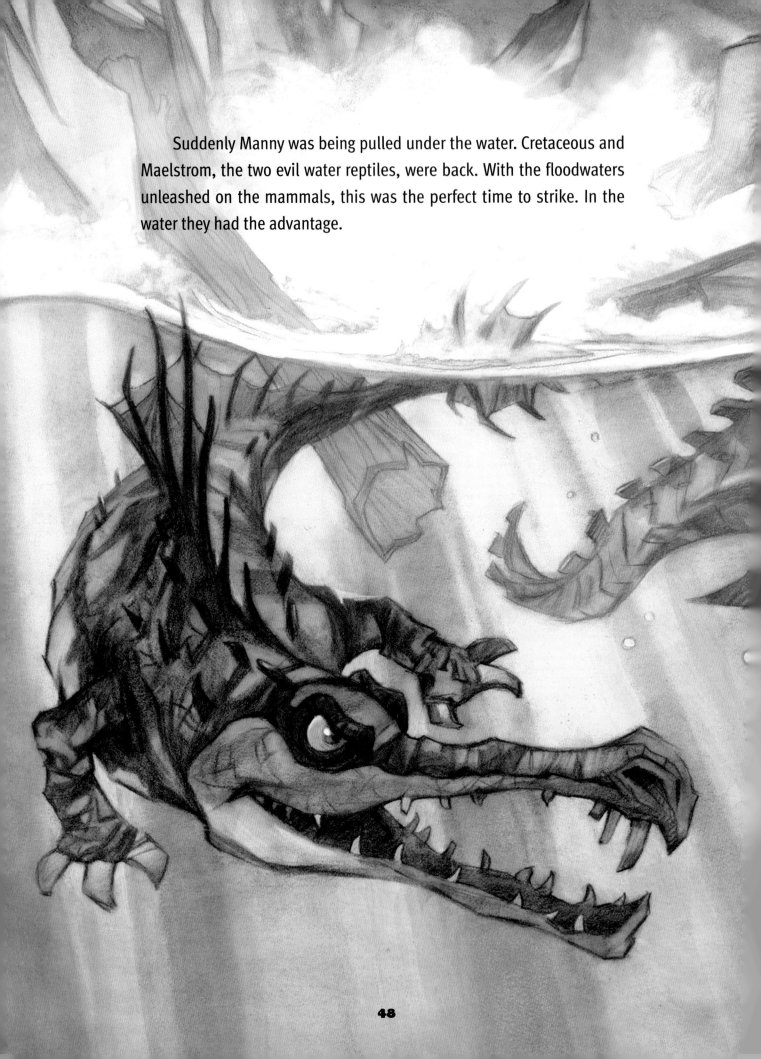

Suddenly Manny was being pulled under the water. Cretaceous and Maelstrom, the two evil water reptiles, were back. With the floodwaters unleashed on the mammals, this was the perfect time to strike. In the water they had the advantage.

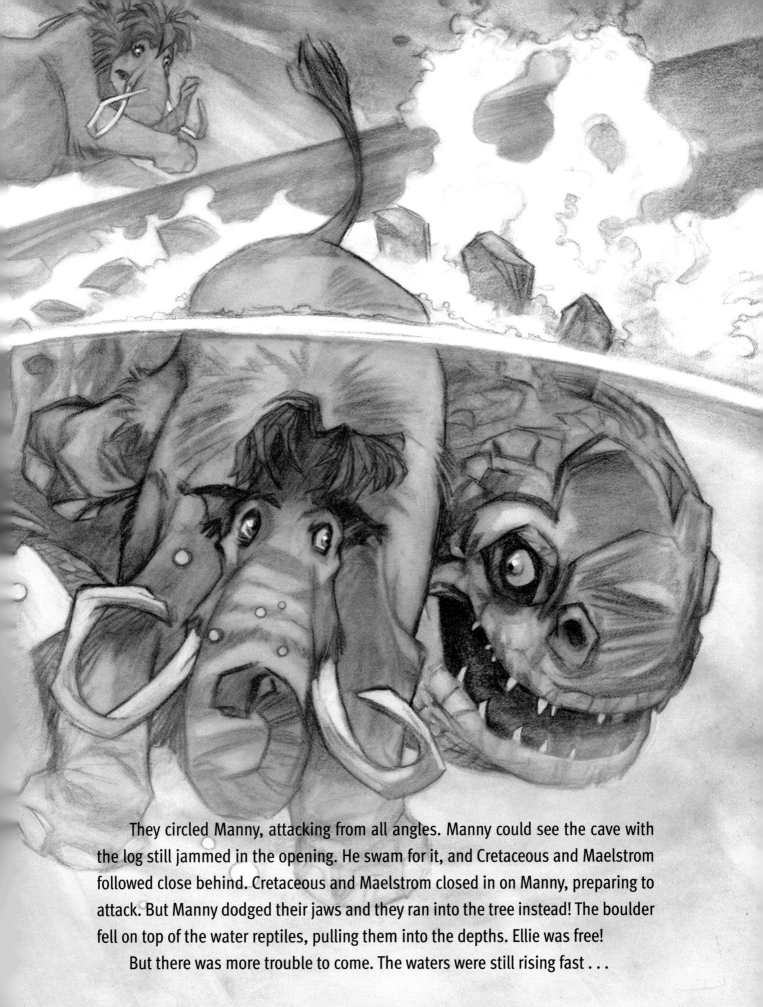

They circled Manny, attacking from all angles. Manny could see the cave with the log still jammed in the opening. He swam for it, and Cretaceous and Maelstrom followed close behind. Cretaceous and Maelstrom closed in on Manny, preparing to attack. But Manny dodged their jaws and they ran into the tree instead! The boulder fell on top of the water reptiles, pulling them into the depths. Ellie was free!

But there was more trouble to come. The waters were still rising fast . . .

Meanwhile, on a nearby glacial wall, hapless Scrat found himself in the wrong place at the wrong time. As he was hunting down a snack, the ice wall he was on suddenly split in two, sending him scrambling.

Then something strange began to happen. The force from the split acted like a vacuum, sucking the floodwaters down like a giant bathtub drain.

In no time the Valley was empty. Where there had been water, there were now only shallow puddles. The huge boat was resting on the valley floor. The animals on the boat let out a huge cheer. The threat from the flood was over.

"Please exit the boat in an orderly fashion," Gustav announced, while animals stampeded past him off the boat.

As Manny, Ellie, and the rest of the friends were enjoying their reunion, they heard a loud trumpeting sound.

Manny and Ellie looked up, awestruck. There in front of them was a majestic herd of mammoths. There *were* more mammoths, and they had found Manny and Ellie!

Ellie turned to Manny. "Well . . . we're not the last ones anymore. . . ."

"So you want to go with them?" Manny asked.

"I am a mammoth. I should probably be with the mammoths. Don't you think?" Ellie said.

Ellie turned to go with the mammoth herd.

Manny didn't want Ellie to go, but when he tried to tell her, he couldn't find the words.

"I hope you find everything you're looking for," he stammered.

They said their good-byes sadly. Ellie went off with the herd, disappointed that Manny would not be joining them.

As Manny watched Ellie go, he realized it was time to move on with his life and he wanted Ellie to be a part of it.

"Go after her," Diego encouraged him.

Manny said good-bye to his best friends, Sid and Diego, then raced off after Ellie and the other mammoths. "Ellie!" he called after her.

Ellie thought she heard something, but when she turned she could see only mammoths in every direction. She left the herd to look around, but still saw nothing. Suddenly, Manny dropped down in front of her. He was hanging by his tail like a possum!

"I want us to be together," he said tenderly. The whole tree bent under his weight, about to snap.

Ellie's eyes lit up, and some mammoths in the herd let out a huge trumpeting cheer.

"Well," Sid said to Diego, "it's just you and me now."

"Fine," Diego replied, eyeing his lazy friend. "But *I* am not going to carry you."

"Oh, c'mon buddy. For old times' sake," Sid begged.

"I'll carry him," a voice boomed, as Sid was lifted off the ground.
Manny was back! And Ellie, Crash, and Eddie were with him.

As the herd of mammoths faded into the horizon, Diego looked at his friend, confused. "But your herd's leaving," he said to Manny.

Manny smiled at the group and replied, "We are a herd now!"

And with the sun setting, the herd of friends walked off together toward a new home and a new life.